A Beginning-to-Read Book

Happy Birthday! Dear Dragon

by Margaret Hillert

Illustrated by Carl Kock

NORWOOD HOUSE PRESS

DEAR CAREGIVER,

The *Beginning-to-Read* series is a carefully written collection of classic readers you may remember from your own childhood. Each book features text comprised of common sight words to provide your child ample practice reading the words that appear most frequently in written text. The many additional details in the pictures enhance the story and offer the opportunity for you to help your child expand oral language and develop comprehension.

Begin by reading the story to your child, followed by letting him or her read familiar words and soon your child will be able to read the story independently. At each step of the way, be sure to praise your reader's efforts to build his or her confidence as an independent reader. Discuss the pictures and encourage your child to make connections between the story and his or her own life. At the end of the story, you will find reading activities and a word list that will help your child practice and strengthen beginning reading skills.

Above all, the most important part of the reading experience is to have fun and enjoy it!

Shannon Cannon

Shannon Cannon,
Literacy Consultant

Norwood House Press • P.O. Box 316598 • Chicago, Illinois 60631
For more information about Norwood House Press please visit our website at
www.norwoodhousepress.com or call 866-565-2900.

LIBRARY OF CONGRESS CATALOGING-IN-PUBLICATION DATA

Hillert, Margaret.
  Happy birthday, dear dragon / by Margaret Hillert ; illustrated by
Carl Kock. — Rev. and expanded library ed.
     p. cm. — (Beginning to read series. Dear dragon)
  Summary: A youngster is delighted with his birthday present,
especially when it helps him do such things as toast marshmallows.
Includes reading activities.
  ISBN-13: 978-1-59953-037-6 (library binding : alk. paper)
  ISBN-10: 1-59953-037-6 (library binding : alk. paper)
  [1. Birthdays—Fiction. 2. Dragons—Fiction.] I. Kock, Carl, ill.
II. Title. III. Series.
PZ7.H558Hap 2007
[E]—dc22   2006007049

This looks good, Mother.
What a big one.
Oh, this is fun.

Here is something.
What is it?
I can not guess.

Oh, look here.
Look at this
    —and this
        —and this!

And here is something that can jump up.

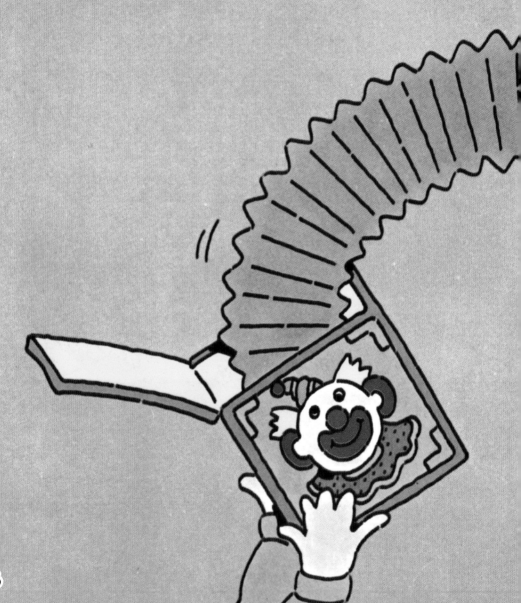

Now come with me.
I want to get you something.
Run, run, run.

Here we go.
In here. In here.
We will look at the dogs.

But we have a dog, Father.
I like the one we have.
I do not want this dog.

Here is something little.
Do you want this?
You can look at it.
It can look at you.

No, I do not like it.
What can it do?
It can not play with me.

Look down here.
You can have this one.
Do you like it?
See it jump.

I like that little one.
But it is not what I want.
Come away.
Come away.

Here is what I want.
Oh, will you get it for me?
I like it.
I like it.
I like it!

Come with me.
Come to my house.
I like you.
We can have fun.

Look, Mother.
See what I have.
It can play with me.

I see. I see.
It is funny.
We will find something for it.

I want to go for a ride.
I will get in.
Help me.
Help me.

Here we go.
Run, run, run.
What fun.
What fun.

Will you do something for me?
Will you help me with this?

Now, *you* have one.
Have two.
Have three.
You are a big help.

Oh, my. Oh, my.
Look what you can do.
I like this.

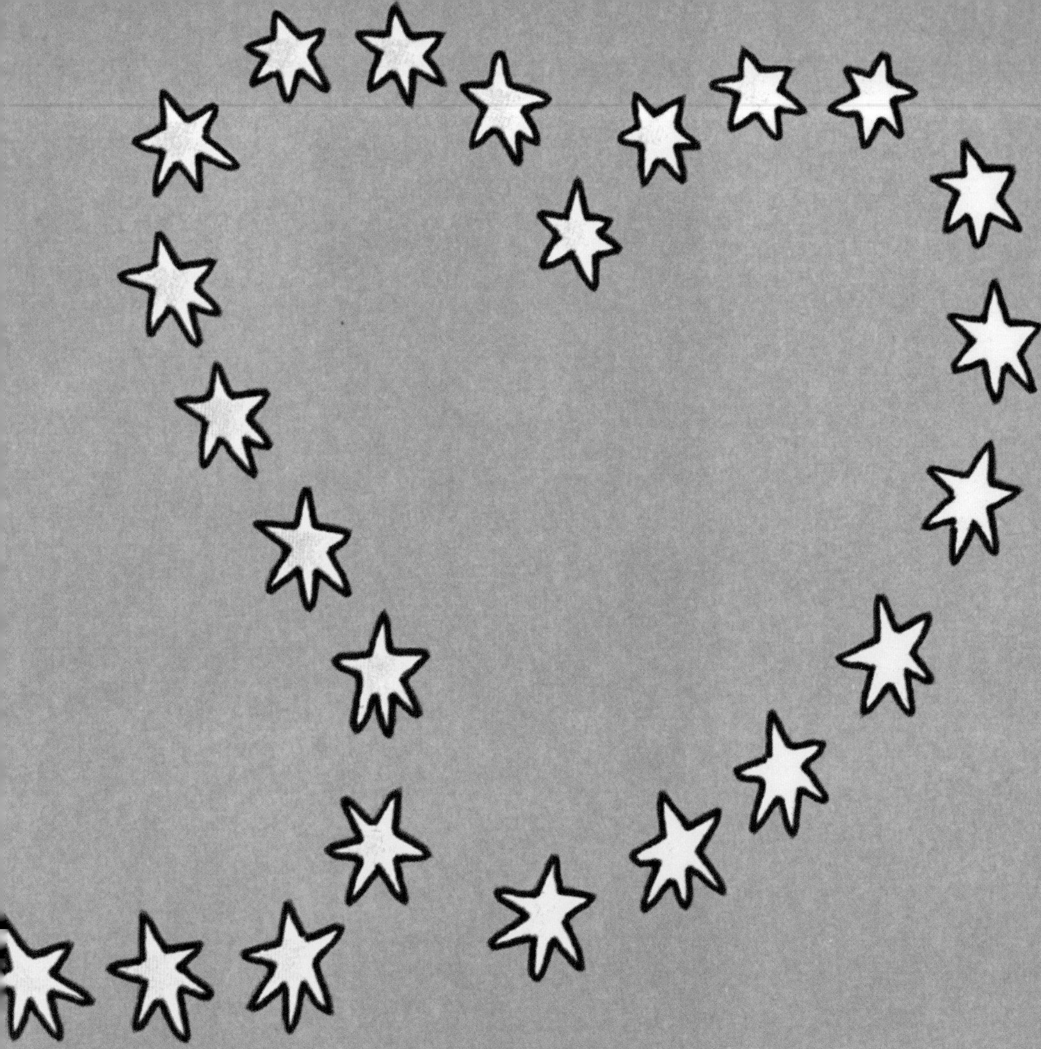

Here you are with me.
And here I am with you.
Oh, what a happy birthday, dear dragon.

The following activities support the findings of the National Reading Panel that determined the most effective components for reading instruction are: Phonemic Awareness, Phonics, Vocabulary, Fluency, and Text Comprehension.

Phonemic Awareness: The /d/ sound

Sound Substitution: Say the words on the left to your child. Ask your child to repeat the word, changing the first sound to /**d**/:

pot - /d/ = dot	junk - /d/ = dunk	keep - /d/ = deep
bent - /d/ = dent	fish - /d/ = dish	near - /d/ = dear
time - /d/ = dime	kid - /d/ = did	rip - /d/ = dip

Phonics: The letter Dd

1. Demonstrate how to form the letters **D** and **d** for your child.
2. Have your child practice writing **D** and **d** at least three times each.
3. Ask your child to point to the words in the book that start with the letter **d**.
4. Write down the following words and ask your child to circle the letter **d** in each word:

do	dragon	dog	dear	day
food	wood	dad	den	hand
riddle	sad	doll	puddle	dig

Vocabulary: Naming Objects

1. Ask your child to tell you different words he or she thinks of that go with "birthday". Write the words on sticky notes and have the child place them next to any objects he or she has named that are in the story.

2. Ask your child to tell a story using all of the words he or she has come up with that relate to birthday.

Fluency: Echo Reading

1. Reread the story to your child at least two more times while your child tracks the print by running a finger under the words as they are read. Ask your child to read the words he or she knows with you.

2. Reread the story, stopping after each sentence or page to allow your child to read (echo) what you have read. Repeat echo reading and let your child take the lead.

Text Comprehension: Discussion Time

1. Ask your child to retell the sequence of events in the story.

2. To check comprehension, ask your child the following questions:

   - Why didn't the boy want the dog for his birthday?
   - Why didn't the boy want the fish for his birthday?
   - Which parts of this story could really happen?
   - Which parts of this story couldn't really happen?
   - Which pet would you choose? Why?

WORD LIST

***Happy Birthday, Dear Dragon* uses the 64 words listed below.**
This list can be used to practice reading the words that appear in the text. You
may wish to write the words on index cards and use them to help your child
build automatic word recognition. Regular practice with these words will
enhance your child's fluency in reading connected text.

a	father	I	oh	up
am	find	in	one	
and	for	is		want
are	fun	it	play	we
at	funny			what
away		jump	ride	will
	get		run	with
big	go	like		
birthday	good	little	see	you
but	guess	look(s)	something	
can	happy	me	that	
come	have	mother	the	
	help	my	this	
dear	here		three	
do	house	no	to	
dog(s)		not	two	
down		now		
dragon				

ABOUT THE AUTHOR Margaret Hillert has written over 80 books for
children who are just learning to read. Her books
have been translated into many different languages and over a million children
throughout the world have read her books. She first started writing poetry as
a child and has continued to write for children and adults throughout her life. A
first grade teacher for 34 years, Margaret is now retired from teaching and lives in
Michigan where she likes to write, take walks in the morning, and care for her three cats.

Photograph by Glenna Washburn

ABOUT THE ADVISER Shannon Cannon contributed the activities pages that appear in
this book. Shannon serves as a literacy consultant and provides
staff development to help improve reading instruction. She is a frequent presenter at educational
conferences and workshops. Prior to this she worked as an elementary school teacher and as
president of a curriculum publishing company.